The Witch's Buttons

by RUTH CHEW

Illustrated by the author

SCHOLASTIC INC.

NEW YORK · TORONTO · LONDON · AUCKLAND · SYDNEY · TOKYO

ISBN 0-590-09840-3

15 14 13 12 11 10 9 8 7 6   7/8

Printed in the U.S.A.   11

To Sandra Rope

1

"OH, Sandy, don't tell me you've already lost a button!" Mrs. James was changing the diaper on Sandy's baby sister. She was tired and cross.

Sandy had just come home from school. She looked down at the brass buttons on her new navy blue coat. There were only five instead of six. "They were all here when I left school. I must have lost it on the way home," she said. "I'll go back and look for it."

Sandy walked the four blocks to school. She was careful to go just the way she had come. She looked among the dry leaves in the gutters, under the parked cars, and all over the sidewalk, but she didn't find the button. At the school Sandy turned around and started back toward home again. She kept on searching for the button.

"What are you looking for?" Janet Kramer had come out of an apartment house on the corner. She was carrying roller skates.

"A button," Sandy said. She wasn't sure she liked Janet. She was a nosy kid, always wanting to know everything, and full of advice.

"Oh," Janet said. "I see. It's off your coat. Those buttons with anchors on them are common. I'll bet we have some in our button bag. Come into my house and I'll look."

Sandy wondered if Janet had meant that the button was cheap, but she followed the other girl through the brick gate into the apartment house.

Janet's apartment was on the first floor. She had a key to her front door. "Mom's still at work," Janet said. She left the skates by the door.

The button bag was in the bottom of a sewing cabinet. It was an old canvas bag filled with dozens of buttons of all kinds. Janet dumped them out onto the kitchen table, and the two girls began to search through them.

"My grandmother used to cut buttons off old clothes and save them," Janet explained. "She gave Mom this bag."

Sandy was so interested in the buttons that she almost forgot to look for one to match those on her coat. Some of the buttons had animals carved on them. Some had pieces of colored glass like jewels. Sandy found one made of bone. It was shaped like a little man.

Janet picked out three brass buttons with anchors on them. The first was too small. The second had a dark background behind the anchor. The ring on the back of the third was broken.

"No luck," Janet said. She began to scoop up the buttons and throw them back into the bag.

Sandy held onto the one shaped like a little man.

"That wouldn't look right on your coat, Sandy," Janet said, "but you can have it if you want it. Maybe you could use it on a Halloween costume."

"Thanks." Sandy put the button into her pocket. "But what shall I do about my coat button?"

"They sell buttons in the trimming store on Thirteenth Avenue," Janet said.

"I have a quarter." Sandy put her hand into her pocket. She felt the quarter, and she felt the button. The button seemed to twist in her hand. She pulled it out and looked at it. There was a grin on the little man's face. Sandy almost dropped the button. "Janet," she whispered, "it's alive!"

"Don't be silly," Janet said. "Come on. We have to get to the trimming store before it closes."

2

THIRTEENTH Avenue in Brooklyn is crowded with all kinds of little stores. Many of them show much of their goods in cardboard boxes on the sidewalk. Sandy and Janet passed stalls of fresh vegetables and stands where dried fish were sold.

On Friday afternoon the Jewish-owned stores close before sundown. The two girls reached the trimming store while it was still open. They walked through the narrow aisles, past the counters covered with gold braid, ball fringe, lace of all colors, and boxes of sequins. At the back of the store a young man with a beard was talking to a little gray-haired woman.

"No," he said. "I don't have any old or unusual buttons. We only stock what is most asked for. You might try an antique shop. Sorry I can't help you." The young man turned to Sandy. "What can I do for you, young lady?"

Sandy pointed to the buttons on her coat. "Please," she said, "do you have a button to match these?"

The young man made his face very solemn. "Well," he said, with a wink at the little gray-haired lady who was still standing at the counter, "I don't know. Those are very rare."

"He thinks he's funny," Janet whispered. "Look at the box on the shelf behind him."

Sandy saw a box with four sizes of

buttons just like hers glued to the side of it. She felt in her pocket for the quarter. By mistake she took out the little bone button that was shaped like a man.

Before she could put the button away, a musical voice said, "Just a minute, please. May I see that?"

It was the little gray-haired woman.
Sandy looked at her. She had a round
face with a curvy mouth, a pointed nose,
and wide-set greeny-blue eyes. She held
out her hand for the button. Sandy
thought she could feel the button squirm.

Sandy held the little button-man up for the woman to see, but she kept a tight grip on it.

The young man with the beard put the box of brass buttons on the counter. "Let's look in here."

Janet fished out one of the right size. "How much is this?" she asked. She nudged Sandy to pay attention.

"They're six for a dollar," the young man said.

"I only need one." Sandy put the button-man back into her pocket and took out the quarter.

The young man smiled. "We'll make it ten cents." He took the quarter and gave Sandy a dime and a nickel change. "Now, if you don't mind, I have to close the store."

The girls left the trimming store. Janet said, "He turned out to be a nice guy after all. Only I wish people wouldn't tease."

Sandy and Janet walked back down Thirteenth Avenue. They passed the carpet store and walked between the tall rolls of linoleum which stood on the sidewalk. When they came to the Italian bakery they stopped to look at the pastry in the window.

"Sandy," Janet whispered, "isn't that the woman who was in the trimming store? Do you think she's following us?"

Sandy looked. The little gray-haired woman was coming toward them. Sandy began to walk fast. Janet ran after her. "What's the matter, Sandy?"

"She wants the magic button," Sandy said.

Janet made a face. "Oh, Sandy!" Then she said, "Anyway, it's a game. Come on. Let's run."

The two girls chased down the busy street, zig-zagging around the barrels of fish and baskets of pumpkins. It was getting dark. No matter how fast they ran the little woman was always right behind them. By the time they reached Sandy's house, both girls were out of breath.

"Bye, Sandy." Janet streaked toward home.

Sandy ran up her front steps and rang the bell. Her mother opened the door. "You were gone a long time," Mrs. James said. "Did you find the button?"

Sandy stepped inside her house, shut the door behind her, and leaned against it. She took the new brass button with the anchor on it out of her pocket and gave it to her mother.

3

AFTER supper Mrs. James said, "Sandy, Daddy and I are going to the movies. I want you to baby-sit for Lisa."

Sandy hated baby-sitting. "Oh, Mother!" she said.

"You should be glad to help your mother, Sandra," Mr. James told her. "She needs a rest sometimes."

"What shall I do if Lisa cries, Mother?" Sandy asked.

"Give her the bottle of milk I have ready in the refrigerator," Mrs. James said. "Be sure to warm it first."

When her mother and father had gone, Sandy tip-toed upstairs to the baby's room to make sure her sister was still asleep. Lisa lay on her stomach. Her eyes were closed. The baby's feet were sticking out from under the pink blanket. Sandy pulled the blanket over them and quietly left the room.

She remembered the little button-man. Sandy had left it in her coat pocket. Her mother had sewn on the new brass button and hung the coat in the hall closet.

Sandy went downstairs to the closet and felt in the coat pocket. The button was still there. She pulled out the little man and looked at it. Each feature of the tiny face was perfect. The little man had a short nose and a long chin. Was he smiling? Sandy couldn't be sure. His clothes looked like those the Pilgrim Fathers wore in Thanksgiving pictures.

Sandy turned the button over. The back was carved just as nicely as the front. In the middle was a loop to sew the button on.

It was an interesting button, but there was really nothing strange about it, Sandy decided. She wondered now why it had seemed magic.

Sandy had an idea. She could wear the button around her neck. She went to the kitchen drawer and found a piece of string. Sandy tried to push the end of the string through the loop on the back of the button. She couldn't get it to go through. At last she took a darning needle from her mother's workbox and threaded it with the string. She poked the needle through the loop and pulled the string after it. Before Sandy could hang the string around her neck, she heard Lisa start to cry.

Sandy ran upstairs to the baby's room. Lisa had rolled over onto her back. Her eyes were still shut, but her mouth was open. Her face was red, and she was howling. When Sandy came into the room the baby opened her eyes and stopped crying for a moment. Then she opened her mouth to start again.

Sandy swung the button on the string in front of the baby. Lisa shut her mouth and made a grab for the button.

The telephone rang downstairs. Sandy tied the string to the top bar of the baby's crib and gave the button a push. It swung gently back and forth.

Sandy ran downstairs to answer the phone. "Hello," she said.

"Hello, Sandy." It was Janet's voice.

"Oh, hi, Janet. I just found a good use for that button you gave me. It keeps my baby sister from crying."

"Be careful she doesn't swallow it," Janet said. "Sandy, it's about that button that I want to talk to you."

"Oh," Sandy said, "you want it back."

"Not exactly," Janet told her. "But, remember the woman who followed us this afternoon? Well, she caught up to me after you went into your house."

"How?" Sandy asked. "You sure were running fast."

There was a silence while Janet thought about this. Then she said, "All I know is she grabbed hold of my arm."

"Weren't you scared?" Sandy asked.

"Scared of what? She's just an old lady who collects buttons — kind of a nice old lady. She wants me to tell you she'll pay five dollars for that button I gave you. It's an antique."

Sandy didn't say anything for a minute. Janet had given her the button without knowing how much it was worth. At last Sandy said, "If you want the button back, Janet, I'll give it to you."

"Oh, Sandy, I didn't say I wanted it back," Janet said. "Now you're mad at me. And we were just getting to be friends."

Sandy heard the baby start to cry. "I have to take care of my sister, Janet," she said. "I'm not mad. Come over tomorrow. We'll decide what to do about the button. Bye." Sandy hung up the telephone and raced upstairs to Lisa's room.

The baby was looking up at the little button-man. He was no longer swinging by the string. Instead he was standing on the top bar of the crib, waving his arms and making faces at the baby.

4

AS soon as Sandy came into the room, the little man toppled off the bar. Once more he was just a button swinging on the end of a string. Lisa stopped screaming.

There was only one thing to do. Sandy walked over to the crib and untied the string from the bar. She held the button up by the string and stared into the tiny face. "There's no use pretending you're just an ordinary button," she said. "I saw you sticking out your tongue at my sister."

The button didn't move. Sandy held it close to her ear. "Can you talk?"

There was no answer.

"Maybe I ought to sell you to the woman who offered five dollars for you," Sandy said.

Suddenly the button gave a sharp twist in her hand. Sandy heard a shriek. "Five dollars! What an insult! Can't you tell that woman is a witch?"

Sandy almost dropped the button. "No need to scream," she said. She held the button in front of her and looked at it.

The little man had his hands on his hips. His eyes flashed under his wide-brimmed hat. He didn't look like a button at all.

"Who are you?" Sandy asked.

The little man didn't answer.

"If you don't want to tell me I may as well sell you to the Witch." Sandy looked to see what effect her words had.

"Oh, I suppose I may as well tell you everything. Only first put me down, and take this rope off me. I feel like a fish

on a line." The little man reached behind him to grab at the string.

Sandy pulled the string out of the loop in the little man's back. She set him down again on the top bar of the crib. The baby watched everything with big dark eyes.

The little button-man sat down on the bar and crossed his legs. "First of all," he said, "my name is Silas. As you may have guessed, I wasn't always a button."

"Why does the Witch want you so much?" Sandy asked.

Silas frowned. "Don't interrupt," he said. "It's rude."

Sandy thought it rude of him to say so, but she waited for him to continue.

He stretched his arms, crossed and

uncrossed his legs several times, fiddled with the wide collar of his coat, and then said, "I was once a person like you."

"What happened?" Sandy asked, forgetting that he didn't like to be interrupted.

Silas didn't answer. He rested his long chin in his hands and seemed to be thinking hard. At last he said, "I spent so many years shut up in that awful button bag that I can hardly remember what happened before." He wrinkled his eyebrows and scratched his head. "I remember that I was sewn to a fur cloak for ages. It never seemed to wear out. That cloak was handed down from mother to daughter to granddaughter. How I hated it. Once long long ago a little boy kept me for a good-luck charm." Silas smiled. "Maybe I *was* lucky for him. He lived to be a very old man, and he always carried me in his waistcoat pocket. I was nearly buried with him, but his granddaughter found me and sewed me to the fur cloak."

This was all interesting, but it didn't answer any of Sandy's questions. She still wanted to know about the Witch.

Silas stood up and yawned. "I've had a tiring day," he said. "Do you have somewhere for me to sleep? And please," he added, "don't put me among buttons."

Suddenly Sandy felt sorry for him. She picked up the little man and carried him down the hall to her bedroom. She put him in the top of the box of Kleenex on her dresser. "How's that?"

Silas snuggled down between two sheets of Kleenex. "Don't wake me early," he said. "I have a lot of sleep to catch up on."

Sandy heard Lisa start to scream. She ran downstairs to warm the milk for the baby.

5

IN the morning when Mrs. James came to wake Sandy, she saw Silas in the Kleenex box. "What's this?" She picked him up. "It's a button. Sandy, wouldn't this be just right for the snowsuit I knitted for Lisa?"

Sandy sat up in bed. "Janet Kramer gave it to me yesterday, Mother. It's an antique and worth a lot. I think I ought to give it back to her."

Mrs. James put Silas down on the dresser top. "Janet called for you already this morning. I told her you weren't awake yet. I wanted you to sleep late after staying up baby-sitting last night." Mrs. James left the room. She had to feed Lisa her breakfast.

Sandy jumped out of bed and began to dress as fast as she could. Before she went downstairs she put Silas into the pocket of her jeans. "Good morning," she whispered.

"Maybe for you it is," came a voice from her pocket. "I could have used a bit more sleep."

"Take a nap in my pocket," Sandy suggested.

After swallowing her orange juice and gobbling a bowl of cereal, Sandy put on an old jacket.

"Where are you going, Sandy?" her mother asked. She was trying to spoon strained peaches into Lisa's mouth. Most of the food seemed to land on the baby's bib or on her chin.

"I'm going to Janet's house, Mother," Sandy said. "I'll be home for lunch."

"All right, Sandy. Have fun." Mrs.

James tried again to get the spoon into the baby's mouth. Lisa grabbed the spoon with both hands. The peaches splashed onto her mother's apron.

Sandy closed the front door behind her. She looked up and down the tree-lined street. There was no sign of the Witch.

Sandy walked the two blocks to the red brick apartment building where Janet lived. Janet was outside, putting on her roller skates. "I'll put these away," she said, "unless you want to go skating, Sandy. I'm sorry I can't ask you to come into the house. Saturday is Mom's house-cleaning day. She likes me to stay out of her way." Janet went into the building and came out a minute later without the skates.

"Where's the Witch?" Sandy asked.

"The Witch?" Janet didn't understand.

"The woman who wants the button," Sandy explained. "I have to tell you what happened last night, Janet. Come on. We'll go for a walk."

"You were using the button to amuse your baby sister," Janet said. "I wish I had a baby sister. My mother won't even let me have a kitten. She says she doesn't have time to take care of one."

"Meow!" A little black kitten ran from under a parked car to rub against Janet's legs. She stooped down and picked it up.

"Oh, Sandy, did you ever see such a pretty kitten?" Janet held the kitten up for Sandy to see.

Sandy looked into a pair of wide-set greeny-blue eyes. She had a funny feeling that she had seen those eyes before.

"Tell me about last night, Sandy." Janet put the kitten on the sidewalk. The two girls started to walk down the street. Sandy looked back. The kitten was following them.

Sandy told Janet all about Silas. Janet listened without saying anything.

"You don't believe me, do you, Janet?" Sandy said. She took Silas out of her pocket and gave him to Janet.

Janet looked hard at the button. She turned it over and looked at the loop on the back. "I don't understand how it can move. There are no joints. It's just a solid piece of bone." She rubbed the little man's stomach.

"Stop that!" Silas said sharply. Janet was so startled that she dropped him.

There was a flash of black fur. The kitten pounced upon the button. She grabbed him in her mouth and raced down the street. The two girls chased after.

The kitten crossed Church Avenue. Luckily the traffic light was green. Sandy and Janet ran across the street.

By the time they had gone three blocks, Sandy had a stitch in her side. She kept on running. Two blocks farther on she noticed an old house. It was different from the other houses on the street. This one was long and low with a chimney on each side. All the windows were boarded up. It didn't look as if anyone lived there.

The kitten ran around to the back of the old house. Sandy and Janet followed. They saw her scramble under a loose board on one of the windows and disappear inside.

6

JANET grabbed hold of the board the kitten had gone under. The wood was rotten, and the board came off in Janet's hand. The board above it was rotten too. Janet pried that one off as well. Now the space was big enough for the two girls to squeeze through.

"I'll go in first," Sandy whispered. She put her finger to her lips. "Try not to make any noise, Janet."

"Why?" Janet asked. "All we have to do is catch the kitten. It should be easier to do in a house than outdoors."

"I'm not sure I want to catch it," Sandy said in a low voice. She remembered now where she had seen those greeny-blue eyes.

"What do you mean?" Janet wanted to know.

"The kitten is the Witch," Sandy explained.

"Oh!" Janet stared at Sandy. "Of course! That's why she grabbed the button. Maybe we shouldn't go into the house, Sandy."

"We have to rescue Silas." Sandy bent down and crawled through the window.

Janet took a deep breath and followed her.

The girls found themselves in a huge old-fashioned kitchen. One whole wall was a stone fireplace. An enormous iron pot hung by a hook over the fire. Something was bubbling and steaming in the pot. The steam rising from it was soft and pink. As the girls watched, it turned to violet, then blue. Suddenly the pot gave a loud hiss. Bright green steam rose in clouds.

Sandy and Janet jumped back. They heard footsteps. Sandy got down on her hands and knees and crawled into a low cupboard. Janet came after her.

The cupboard smelled good. There was a basket of apples back in one corner. Janet left the cupboard door open a crack so that she and Sandy could peek out.

Someone was singing in a sweet voice. The little gray-haired woman they had met in the button shop came dancing into the room. She was dressed all in black now. Sandy noticed that her little feet were in shoes with big buckles on them. They were a lot like the shoes that Silas wore. The Witch seemed excited. She twirled all around the big kitchen.

"Stop it, Betsy!" It was Silas' voice. "You're up to something. I can tell by the way you're acting."

Now Janet and Sandy saw that the Witch was holding the little button-man in her hand. He was kicking and struggling.

The Witch walked over to the steaming pot. She looked into it. "Yes, yes, it's nearly at the right stage." She hummed for a minute. Then she said, "Now, now, Silas, this will all be over in a moment."

The girls watched in horror as the Witch dropped Silas into the pot. There was a bang like a firecracker. The room filled with clouds of black smoke. Sandy and Janet put their hands over their mouths. They could hear the Witch coughing.

"Oh, dear," she said. "I wish I could find a better method. How is it going, Silas?"

"How should I know?" they heard Silas say. "You and your sloppy spells!" His voice seemed very loud.

The smoke was clearing. Sandy blinked her eyes. She grabbed Janet's hand and whispered, "Look!"

Something big and wet was rising out of the huge pot. Now the girls saw that it was a man. He wore a wide-brimmed hat and knee breeches. It was Silas!

7

THE Witch clapped her hands. When Silas had climbed out of the pot she danced around and around him. "It worked! It worked!" she sang. "I wasn't sure it would."

"What would you have done if it hadn't?" Silas snarled.

"Now, now, Silas. It took me ages to put together that brew. I had to melt some of my nicest buttons into it."

"Good of you, dear sister," Silas said. "But if you hadn't turned me into a button in the first place, you wouldn't have had to go to so much trouble to change me back."

The Witch put her hand on her brother's arm. "Let's have no hard feelings, Silas," she said. "I did it for your own good. I thought it would teach you a lesson. You were always meddling with my button collection. I meant to change you back to yourself after a week. How was I to know that horrid little boy would find you and put you into his pocket? I followed him around for years trying to get you away from him. And you didn't help."

Silas shook her hand off. He glared at his sister. "I couldn't be sure what you would do if you got your hands on me. At least the boy kept me safe." He looked around the kitchen. "A fine state you've let the house get into, Betsy. All you ever think of are your precious buttons."

The Witch caught sight of the window from which Janet had pulled the two boards. "I must have knocked those

boards off when I came in," she said.
"I was rather in a hurry. You'll find the
hammer and the nails where we always
kept them, Silas. Make yourself useful."

He glared. "After three hundred years
as a button, I'm supposed to be useful!
I never did like this old house. It can
fall apart for all I care."

"You know I didn't *have* to change
you back," the Witch said. Then she
laughed. "Oh, if only you could have
seen your face when I held you over the
pot! What did you think I was going to
do to you?"

"Nothing I wouldn't do to you, dear
sister," Silas muttered. He stamped out
of the kitchen.

Witch Betsy hummed to herself for a
minute. Then she said, "Oh, dear, I hope
he doesn't find my buttons." She chased
after her brother.

"Quick!" Sandy whispered. "We've got

to get out of here before they nail those boards back."

Janet crawled first out of the cupboard, and Sandy scrambled after her. The two girls stood up and ran to the window. A moment later they were outside. They tore around the house to the street and ran toward home.

After they crossed Beverly Road they slowed down. And while they were waiting for the Church Avenue traffic light to change, Sandy pulled two red apples out of the front of her jacket. She grinned. "I swiped these. After all, Witch Betsy swiped our button."

Janet looked at Sandy with admiration. "Wow!" she said. "You sure have a lot of nerve." She took one of the apples and bit into it. "Delicious," she said.

Sandy crunched her way through the other apple. It was hard and sweet and tasted better than anything she could remember. When she finished it she wiped her mouth with the back of her hand.

The traffic light had changed now. Sandy crossed the street and looked around for Janet. She didn't see her anywhere.

Sandy waited for a minute. Then she walked back across Church Avenue to look for her friend. Funny. Where could Janet have gone?

Sandy had begun to like Janet. This was such a stupid trick. Maybe Janet thought it was funny, but Sandy didn't. Once again she crossed the busy street and walked slowly home.

8

SANDY walked up the front steps of her house and rang the doorbell. Mrs. James opened the door and looked out. Then she frowned and shut the door.

Sandy didn't know what to think. Either her mother had gone crazy or she had gone blind. Both these thoughts were scary, but Mrs. James didn't seem to have even noticed Sandy.

She decided to ring the bell again. This time she meant to walk into the house before her mother could close the door. If there was something wrong with her mother somebody had to take care of the baby.

Sandy tried to feel brave. She looked at the push button for the bell and then put her finger on it. But Sandy didn't press the button. She just stared at it. Now she knew what was wrong. She couldn't see her finger!

Sandy looked down at where she knew her jacket was. She couldn't see it, or her jeans, or her feet. If she couldn't see herself, her mother couldn't either. Sandy was invisible!

What could have happened? Sandy sat down on her front steps and thought for a long time. She tried to remember everything that had taken place that morning. Did the Witch know somehow that Sandy was hiding in her kitchen? In some way she had enchanted her. Was Janet enchanted too?

Of course Janet was invisible too! She hadn't hidden from Sandy. Most likely she thought Sandy had hidden from her.

Janet must have gone home alone too. But Janet had a key to her front door.

Sandy stood up and started to walk to the apartment building where Janet lived. It felt strange to pass people she knew and not have them say hello. She saw Jerry Meyer who sat beside her in school. He was always hiding her eraser or turning the pages in her reader so she'd lose her place.

Sandy grabbed Jerry's cap and ran down the street. Jerry chased after the cap. Sandy dodged back and forth with it. She put it on the sidewalk and waited.

When Jerry reached for the cap, Sandy snatched it up. Jerry's mouth was open. His eyes were popping out. Sandy thought he looked just like a frog. She ran around the corner and hid the cap on a windowsill. Jerry looked everywhere for it. Finally Sandy picked up the cap and set it on Jerry's head. She pulled it down over his eyes and walked away.

Sandy went into Janet's apartment building and rang Janet's bell. Janet's mother opened the door. Sandy ducked under Mrs. Kramer's arm and rushed into the hall of the apartment. She spread her arms wide and walked around all the rooms as if she were an airplane. This way, she told herself, even if she couldn't see Janet, she'd be sure to bump into her.

Mrs. Kramer shut the front door and muttered, "They're rushing Halloween."

Sandy found one door that was shut. She opened it quietly and went in, closing the door behind her. She was in a frilly pink and white bedroom with a four-poster bed in the middle. It was just the sort of room Sandy had always longed for.

She noticed a hollow in the middle of the bed.

"Janet!" Sandy whispered.

The bedsprings creaked.

"Oh, Sandy, is it you? What's happened?" Janet's voice said.

Sandy sat down on the bed. "We're invisible, Janet. The Witch must have enchanted us."

"But how, Sandy? We were all right when we left her house. It wasn't till we got to Church Avenue that anything happened. I looked around for you, and you were gone."

Sandy was quiet for a minute. Then she said, "Janet, do you suppose it could have been those apples I swiped?"

"Maybe," Janet said. "The important thing is: What are we going to do about it?"

Sandy looked around the pretty room. There was a pink telephone on the white and gold table near the bed. "Janet, may I use your phone?" Sandy asked.

"Of course. Are you going to call Witch Betsy and ask her to take off the enchantment?"

"No," Sandy said, "but it's not a bad idea." She took the receiver off the hook and dialed her home number.

Her mother answered the phone.

"Hello, Mother," Sandy said. "I'm at Janet's house. Please may I stay here for lunch?"

"All right, Sandy," her mother said, "but don't be late for supper."

9

SANDY hung up the telephone. She told Janet what had happened when she tried to go home. "At least this way my mother won't worry when I don't come home for lunch," she said. "What about your mother, Janet? Won't she wonder where you are?"

Sandy heard the bedsprings creak again. The hollow in the bed became flat. A chair moved back from the desk in the corner of the room. The pen on top of the desk flew up into the air and then settled, point down, on the desk top. It started to write on a sheet of paper.

"I'm writing a note for Mom," Janet said. "I'll leave it on the kitchen table. Come on. We'll get something to eat before we go."

"Where are we going?" Sandy asked.

"To see Witch Betsy, of course," Janet said. "I'm sure she'll help us. She doesn't seem like a bad witch at all. If you want to know, I like her a lot better than that nasty brother of hers."

Sandy wanted to be loyal to Silas, but deep inside her she felt that Janet was right.

The girls tip-toed out of the bedroom and went to the kitchen. Mrs. Kramer was in the living room, vacuuming the rug. She didn't notice the door of Janet's room open and then close again.

Janet put the note she had written on the kitchen table. She took a container of milk out of the refrigerator and filled two glasses. Then she opened a fresh loaf of bread and pulled out four slices. "Hope you like baloney." She made two sandwiches. Janet handed one sandwich to Sandy and took a bite out of the other.

The girls sat down at the kitchen table and ate as fast as they could. Suddenly the sound of the vacuum cleaner stopped. They could hear footsteps.

"Drink up your milk and hide your sandwich," Janet whispered.

Sandy stuffed her sandwich into her pocket. As soon as it was inside her clothes it became invisible too. Janet's mother came into the kitchen just as Sandy was putting her empty glass on the table.

Mrs. Kramer stared. She walked over to the table and saw Janet's note.

Dear Mom,

    I am invisible, but otherwise healthy. Don't worry about me. You'll see me just as soon as I get to be visible again.

                Love,
                Janet

Mrs. Kramer looked at the two empty milk glasses on the table. "I was sure I saw one of them move," she said to herself. She read Janet's note again. She put her hand to her forehead. "I'm tired, and my head hurts. I'd better take a nap." Mrs. Kramer went to her room to lie down.

Sandy and Janet finished eating their sandwiches and left the apartment.

10

"THAT'S funny." Sandy looked at the back window of the Witch's house. "The two boards are still off."

"Betsy was after Silas to nail them back," Janet said. "He's had plenty of time to do it."

Sandy grabbed Janet by the arm. "Listen!"

They could hear loud footsteps inside the house. A door banged. Then there was a crash. Someone said something in a harsh voice. It sounded like Silas.

"Maybe we shouldn't go in right now," Janet said. "It sounds as if they're having a fight."

The big yard of the old house was overgrown with weeds. Sandy and Janet crouched down in them. A moment later

someone banged off another board from the kitchen window. Silas came bursting out. His wide-brimmed hat fell off his head. He had to stoop over to pick it up.

Janet and Sandy held their breath. Silas was very tall now. His clothes were black, and his face was red and angry. "Don't worry, sister dear, I'll find the rest of your buttons," he said. He didn't seem to be talking to himself, but the girls couldn't see anyone else. Silas stamped through the weeds to the front of the house. They saw him turn and

go down the street toward Church Avenue.

"I'm glad he's gone," Janet said. "Now let's talk to Witch Betsy. By the way, Sandy, why are we hiding? We're invisible."

"Oh," Sandy said. "I forgot."

They stepped over the windowsill into the kitchen. It was much easier to get into the house now that Silas had knocked off another board.

The fire had gone out under the big pot. Sunlight poured into the kitchen through the unboarded window. The big room looked quite different.

Janet led the way out of the kitchen. They found themselves in a hall with a room on each side of it. They peeked through the doorways. The rooms were furnished with plain, old-fashioned furniture. One room was a parlor. The other was a dining room. They were covered with dust and cobwebs as if nobody ever used them any more. Both rooms had fireplaces, but they looked as if nobody had made a fire in them for many years.

A big staircase led up from the hall near the front door. Janet put her hand on the bannister. It wobbled. She started up the stairs, one step at a time, listening for any sound upstairs. On the landing she stopped and waited for Sandy to catch up with her.

"Maybe we ought to call the Witch," Sandy said. "Even if we are invisible, I'm not sure I want to surprise her. She might do something she'd be sorry for later. Remember what she did to Silas."

Janet nodded, forgetting that Sandy couldn't see her nod. She swallowed once. Then she called in a low voice, "Betsy!"

No answer.

Now Sandy called, louder, "Betsy,

please come out. You can't see us, but we're on the stairs. We want to talk to you."

Still no answer. The girls went upstairs. There was a sudden rustle and the sound of scurrying feet. Something ran across the upstairs hall and into one of the rooms. Janet jumped. Then she laughed. "It's only a mouse."

There were four rooms opening off the hall. Sandy and Janet peeked into all of them. They looked as if a frantic search had been going on. Chairs were overturned. Drawers were pulled out onto the floor. The covers had been yanked off the beds. The girls couldn't see the Witch anywhere.

Sandy opened a door in the corner of the back bedroom. She found a narrow stair. With Janet close behind her, holding onto her jacket, Sandy went down the steps. When she opened the door at the bottom they walked into the kitchen.

"Now what do we do?" Janet asked.

Sandy walked over to the big pot. She leaned over it and sniffed. "It smells like nail polish remover."

There was a small blue bottle with a cork in it on a shelf above the fireplace. Sandy uncorked the bottle and dipped it into the pot. She filled it to the brim and stuffed the cork back. Then she put the bottle into the pocket of her jeans.

"Nail polish remover is good for all sorts of things," she said. "Did you know it will take off the stickum left by a Band-Aid?"

"I can't stand the smell of nail polish remover," Janet said. She dipped her finger into the pot and then looked at it. "It doesn't work either."

"Of course not," Sandy told her. "It's cold. Are there any matches here?"

"Witch Betsy probably rubs two sticks together to make a fire," Janet said.

"No, she doesn't." Sandy held up a box of wooden kitchen matches. "We're in luck, but even with these I'm not sure I can get a fire started."

There was a box of wood in one corner of the kitchen. Janet had spent two weeks at Girl Scout Camp last summer. She showed Sandy how to make a fire without newspaper.

Sandy watched with interest. She couldn't see Janet at all, and the sticks of wood seemed to move by themselves. Soon the fire was crackling. As it burned higher, the brew in the big iron pot started to bubble. Then a pale gray steam began to rise from it.

Moments later the steam had turned pink, then violet, then blue. With the loud hiss they remembered, the pot poured forth bright green steam.

"I think it's ready," Janet said in a shaky voice, "but I don't want to get into that pot. Suppose something went wrong? I'd be boiled alive."

Sandy took a long handled spoon from a hook over the fireplace. She dipped the spoon into the brew and splashed a drop onto the back of her hand, just as she did when she tested the baby's milk. When the drop of brew touched her hand it made a little popping sound. The liquid felt cool.

"Oh, Janet, look!" Sandy said. "It works!" She held up her hand. A little pink round spot of Sandy was visible.

"I don't care," Janet said. "I'm not going to mess around with that stuff."

"It's not hot, Janet. Feel it." Sandy dipped the spoon into the pot and splashed a large spoonful of the brew in the direction of Janet's voice.

There was a crackling like a string of

firecrackers going off. Suddenly parts of Janet were visible. Sandy could see a bit of Janet's red jacket, the bottom half of her left ear, part of a shoelace, and one angry eye.

"Warn me before you do that again," Janet said. "You're wasting the brew this way, Sandy. If we run out of it, I'll be a walking jigsaw puzzle."

"You're right, Janet," Sandy said. "We'd better just get into the pot." She closed her mouth and squinched her eyes shut. "Here goes." Sandy stepped into the steaming brew.

Bang! The room was filled with black smoke. Janet didn't know whether to cough or to scream. She decided not to do either. Seconds later she watched Sandy come dripping but visible out of the brew.

Janet took a deep breath and stepped into the pot.

11

SANDY was home in plenty of time for supper. Her mother looked very happy. She opened the door and gave Sandy a hug.

"Did you have a good day, Sandy?" she asked.

"Yes," Sandy said. "I like Janet Kramer."

"Maybe she'll come over tonight and keep you company when you baby-sit. I know it isn't fair to ask you to do it two nights in a row, but the Thompsons asked us over. We haven't been to see them in ages."

Sandy walked into the house and closed the front door. Her mother went on talking. "You and Janet can bake cookies if you want to."

"Oh, could I, Mother? That would be great." Sandy loved to cook.

"I'll ask Janet's mother to let her spend the night." Mrs. James walked over to the telephone. "What's her number?"

Sandy told her mother Janet's telephone number. She took off her jacket and went to hang it in the hall closet. When she came back her mother was humming and setting the table. "Janet is coming over for supper," Mrs. James said. "Shall we use the good china?"

Supper was like a party. Both Sandy's father and Janet told jokes. Lisa sat in her high chair and chewed on a piece of zwieback and didn't scream even once.

While everybody but Lisa was eating apple pie, Mrs. James said, "I had a piece of good luck this afternoon. A man came to the house selling buttons. Usually I don't bother with people like that, but he was so strange looking that I felt sorry for him. I don't think he was quite right in the head. Well, the very first thing he showed me was exactly what I need for the snowsuit I made for Lisa. It's a bit like that button Janet gave you, Sandy. Just think, the poor man only wanted to charge me a penny. I gave him a quarter for it."

"Is that why you were so happy this

afternoon, Mother?" Sandy asked. "I'm glad you got a button you like."

"Funny thing. The man made me promise to sew the button onto the snowsuit right away. But I just haven't had the time. I'll sew it on tomorrow." Mrs. James poured herself a second cup of coffee.

When dinner was over, Janet and Sandy started to load the dishwasher.

"Leave the pans," Mrs. James said. "I'll scrub them in the morning." She carried Lisa upstairs to bed and then went to get her hat and coat. Mr. James was all ready to go. He was waiting for her in the front hall.

When her parents had gone out, Sandy said, "Lisa ought to start crying any minute now. She just waits for my mother to leave."

"I don't hear anything," Janet said.

"Don't be silly, Sandy. She's a darling baby."

Sandy closed the dishwasher and turned it on. "We'll sneak upstairs and see if she's asleep."

Silently the two girls crept upstairs to the baby's room. Mrs. James had left a little lamp on, and the door was open.

Sandy and Janet heard someone singing a lullaby in a low sweet voice. They peeked into the room. Lisa lay on her stomach in the crib. They could see that her eyes were almost closed. In a moment she would be asleep.

The new snowsuit was on top of the dresser. Right beside it stood a little figure.

Her clothes weren't black any more, and she seemed to be made of bone. But there was no doubt who it was. Witch Betsy was singing the baby to sleep.

12

SANDY opened her mouth to say something. Witch Betsy saw her and put her finger to her lips. Lisa's eyelashes fluttered and then lay still on her cheeks. The baby was asleep.

Betsy walked to the edge of the dresser and looked down. It was a long way to the floor. She held out her arms the way Lisa did when she wanted to be picked up. Janet tip-toed into the room and gently lifted the little Witch. She carried her downstairs.

Sandy walked over to the crib to make

sure that her sister was all right. Lisa seemed to be having a happy dream. She smiled in her sleep.

Sandy had read stories about witches who stole babies. When she went downstairs she found Janet in the kitchen. Witch Betsy was sitting on the edge of the table, swinging her legs.

"You must like babies a lot to turn yourself into a button for a baby's snowsuit," Sandy said to the Witch.

"I don't like babies any more than you do," Betsy said. "Babies like to be sung to, and I like to sing. Anyway, I didn't turn myself into a button. That copycat little brother of mine did it to me."

"Is Silas a witch too?" Sandy asked.

"Not a good one," Witch Betsy said. "He never thinks up his own spells, but he sometimes remembers mine."

"How did he turn you into a button?" Janet asked.

"I'd better not tell you," the Witch said. "It's so easy you might want to try it. The hard part is turning a button back into a person."

"But you don't seem to mind being a button," Sandy said.

Betsy climbed up onto the rim of a small saucepan that was on the table. Holding her arms out, she balanced herself like a tight-rope walker. "In some ways it's fun," the Witch said. "But once I'm sewn onto something I won't be able to move. I'll be just like any other button." Betsy balanced herself for a few steps. Suddenly she jumped down onto the tabletop. She stretched herself out on her stomach and buried her face in her hands. Her tiny shoulders shook. The Witch was crying.

Sandy couldn't bear it. "Don't cry," she said. "I'm sure we can do something to help you."

"Of course we can, Sandy," Janet said. "We can take Betsy back to her house and drop her into the pot of brew."

The Witch stopped crying. She sat up and wiped her eyes on the hem of her skirt. "You have to be careful of Silas," she said. "The way I am I wouldn't be able to help you. And what would we do if Silas turned both of you into buttons?"

Sandy was very quiet. She knew just how to help the Witch. But she remembered how happy her mother was to have the right button for Lisa's snowsuit. No matter what Sandy did, someone was going to be unhappy.

Sandy thought hard. She tried to imagine what it would be like for Betsy to be sewn onto the snowsuit and not to be able to move — or sing.

Sandy pulled the little blue bottle out of her pocket. She uncorked it and poured the brew into the little saucepan on the table. The smell of nail polish remover filled the room.

Witch Betsy clapped her hands and danced a jig on the tabletop. She watched as Sandy put the saucepan on the stove and turned on the burner.

Soon the magic brew bubbled. The steam began to change color. Sandy picked up the Witch and got ready to drop her into the saucepan.

"Sandy, stop!" Janet yelled. "You don't want a full-sized witch on top of your stove!"

Sandy put the pan from the apple pie on the floor. She set the Witch in the middle of it and poured the steaming brew over her.

13

THERE wasn't enough brew to make a very loud bang when Sandy poured it over the Witch. But it was loud enough to wake the baby. Before the black smoke cleared Lisa started to cry. Sandy ran out of the kitchen and hurried upstairs.

Lisa had rolled over onto her back. She was reaching out her arms toward the dresser top and howling. Sandy thought that it wasn't just her mother who would miss the magic button. Lisa missed it already.

Sandy picked up the baby and started to walk back and forth with her. Usually this made Lisa stop crying. Now she only screamed louder.

"Rock-a-bye baby, on the tree-top," a sweet voice sang. Lisa stopped crying and turned her head to see where the voice came from.

Betsy, dressed in black and back to her usual size, had come into the room. Janet was right behind her.

"I see what you mean about that baby, Sandy," Janet said. "I never thought anybody so small could make so much noise."

"She wants the magic button," Sandy explained.

Betsy stopped singing. "I never thought of that." She frowned. "Well, I can't spend all my time singing to your sister, Sandy. I have to go home and take care of my buttons. Silas found most of them, but I hid the best ones. I know he's going to keep on looking for them. Silas is such a nuisance."

"Turn him back into a button," Janet suggested.

"Can't," the Witch said. "The spell only works once."

"If that's how it is," Janet said, "Silas can't turn you into a button anymore either."

Betsy smiled. "No, he can't."

Sandy was still walking up and down with the baby. Lisa had forgotten the button. She liked having people around her. The baby began to feel heavy to Sandy. She put her back into the crib. Lisa let out a yowl.

Janet leaned over Lisa and tickled her. "Let me mind her, Sandy."

Betsy straightened one of her gray curls and shook out her full skirt. "I'd better be getting along home. Thank you both for helping me."

"I wish you could stay," Sandy said. "Janet and I are going to make cookies."

"Cookies?" the Witch said. "I haven't made cookies since Silas and I moved from Salem. Maybe I will stay."

The pie pan was still on the kitchen floor. Most of the brew had steamed away. Sandy picked up the pie pan and set it on the kitchen table.

Janet put Lisa in her high chair so she could watch what was going on. Then Janet began to look through the cookbook. Sandy got out the flour, sugar, eggs, and butter. She turned on the oven

and took a cooky sheet and two cooky cutters out of the cupboard.

Betsy was looking at everything in the kitchen. "Where's your rolling pin?" she asked.

"I use a soda bottle," Sandy said. She took one out of the refrigerator and handed it to the Witch.

Betsy began to sing, "Run, run, as fast as you can. You can't catch me. I'm a gingerbread man!"

Janet had found a recipe she liked. The girls mixed the dough and rolled it

between two sheets of waxed paper. Then they cut it into shapes with the cooky cutters. Sandy made rabbits, and Janet made stars.

Betsy gathered up the scraps that were left from the rabbits and stars. She pounded them into a little ball and dipped it into the pie pan. Then she pinched and squeezed it.

Sandy and Janet laid their cookies on the cooky sheet. Sandy put it into the oven. Just before she closed the oven door, Betsy stuck her lump of dough on one corner of the cooky sheet.

"Nail polish remover — ick!" Janet whispered to Sandy. "Remind me not to eat *that* one."

Betsy dusted her hands. She looked at the kitchen clock. "I'd better leave before your mother and father come home, Sandy." She smiled. "I haven't had so much fun in years. Good-bye." The Witch walked to the front door. Janet and Sandy heard it close behind her.

Lisa was fast asleep in the high chair. She didn't wake when Sandy picked her up and carried her upstairs. Janet kept watch over the cookies while Sandy put the baby into her crib.

When Sandy came back into the kitchen the cookies were nice and brown. Janet opened the oven door. With a pot-holder, Sandy pulled out the cooky sheet. She set it on the table to cool.

The girls leaned over the cooky sheet to admire their rabbits and stars, but all either of them saw was the cooky the Witch had made. It looked like a button, and it seemed to be made of bone. And it was exactly like Witch Betsy!

As soon as it was cool, Sandy took the Witch's cooky upstairs. She put it on the dresser in Lisa's room, beside the snowsuit.

14

SANDY and Janet whispered together for hours after they went to bed. They slept late next morning.

Janet woke first. She sat up in bed and rubbed her eyes. The sunlight was streaming through the tall bay windows in Sandy's room.

Mrs. James looked into the room. "Good morning, Janet. Your mother telephoned, and I told her you were still asleep. She and your father have to go to a wedding today. I told her you could spend the day with Sandy."

Sandy was awake now. She jumped out of bed and gave her mother a hug. "That's great!" she said. She noticed that her mother was holding the snowsuit. "Did you sew on the button?"

Mrs. James held up the snowsuit. "Yes, doesn't it look nice? Just imagine, the man who sold it to me rang the bell this morning. I thought he wanted the button back, but he only wanted to be sure I'd sewn it onto something. I showed him the snowsuit. He was so pleased that he insisted on giving me a basket of apples. Poor man, I'm sure there's something wrong with him."

Sandy pulled off her pajamas and started to dress. "Apples! Where are they, Mother?"

"In the kitchen. I was tempted to eat one, but I think I'll make a pie and maybe some applesauce for the baby. You'll see the apples when you get your breakfast. Make yourself some waffles. I have batter ready in a pitcher on the kitchen table. And the waffle iron is hot." Mrs. James went down the hall to the baby's room.

The girls dressed in a hurry and ran downstairs. The basket of apples was on the kitchen floor.

"What's the matter, Sandy?" Janet asked. "Why are you so excited?" She picked up one of the apples and smelled it. "M-m-m."

Sandy snatched the apple away from her and threw it back into the basket. "Are you out of your mind, Janet? Don't you remember what these apples did to us? And my mother wants to feed them to the baby!"

Janet looked at her. "You mean," she said, "they're the Witch's apples?"

"Of course," Sandy said. "Don't you recognize the basket? Help me, Janet."

Sandy took one side of the basket and
Janet held the other. Together they
managed to carry the heavy basket to the
hall closet. Sandy shoved it behind the
vacuum cleaner and threw her last year's

coat over it. "I'll have to get it out of here later," she whispered, "but this ought to do for now."

Janet quietly closed the closet door. The girls went back to the kitchen to eat breakfast.

"Betsy's right," Janet said. "Silas is a nuisance." She opened the waffle iron.

Sandy poured the batter into the iron. "We'd better go to see the Witch before he does anything else."

The waffles were delicious. It seemed a shame to have to eat them in such a hurry, but neither Sandy nor Janet wanted to be around when Mrs. James started to look for the apples. They finished breakfast and stacked their dishes in the dishwasher. Then they put on their jackets.

Sandy called upstairs, "It's a lovely day, Mother. We're going out."

"Have fun," Mrs. James said.

15

"I WONDER what Silas will think when he sees Betsy," Janet said. "Your mother showed him the cooky button sewn to the snowsuit."

"Why didn't he see Betsy when she went home last night?" Sandy wanted to know.

Sandy and Janet crossed Church Avenue and walked down the street toward the old house.

"Do you think we should knock on the front door or sneak in by the back window?" Janet asked.

"I don't think anybody ever uses that front door," Sandy said.

The girls crossed three more streets and headed down the long block where the Witch's house stood.

"Sandy!" Janet gasped. "Look!"

Sandy couldn't believe her eyes. There must have been a terrible fire last night. Where the old house had been was only a blackened ruin. The brick chimneys were still standing, but not much else was left of the house. A few charred boards were all that was left of the walls. The weeds had been trampled flat by the firemen. Broken panes of glass from the windows littered the ground. Still hanging from its hook was the great iron pot.

Sandy had an awful thought. "Betsy must have been asleep in the house."

"I know," Janet said in a low voice.

The two girls picked their way through the crushed weeds and piles of shattered glass. They stepped into what had once been the parlor. The mantelpiece had been smashed by a fireman's ax. There was a hole in the chimney. Sandy saw something gleaming inside.

She got down on her hands and knees and crawled into the fireplace. Reaching up, she grabbed hold of an object that was jammed up into the chimney and held in place by two spikes hammered into the bricks. Sandy tried jiggling it to get it loose, but it was wedged tight. Soot and ashes poured down on her.

Sandy coughed and backed out of the fireplace. "There's something hidden in the chimney, Janet. Can you reach it through the hole?"

"I'm not tall enough," Janet said. "Maybe if I stood on your back I could get it."

Sandy crouched down. "I'm filthy already," she said. "Go ahead." She braced herself.

Janet stepped on Sandy's back. She reached into the hole in the chimney. "Got it," she said. She lifted out the object and stepped down.

Sandy stood up and shook herself. "You weigh more than I thought." She brushed her hair out of her eyes. "What did you fish out?"

"A little chest," Janet said.

"It looks like gold." Sandy rubbed the metal box.

"Brass," Janet said. She shook the chest. It rattled.

Sandy looked around. "Let's get away from here. Silas may be back at any time. We know *he* wasn't in the house when it burned. My mother saw him this morning."

Janet shoved the brass chest under her jacket. "We'll go to my house. Mom and Dad won't be back from that wedding for hours."

On the way to Janet's house they kept looking for Silas, but they didn't see him anywhere. They walked as fast as they could. Neither of them felt like talking.

Sandy was trying not to think about Betsy.

At last they came to the red brick apartment building. When Janet unlocked her front door, the two girls went right to the frilly pink bedroom. Janet took the little brass chest out from under her jacket and put it on the bed. Then she and Sandy sat down, one on each side of the chest, to look at it.

The chest was carved with a strange pattern of twisting, curling shapes. Sandy thought they were leaves, but they looked more like feathers to Janet. Although the brass was smooth and worn as if by long years of use, the hinges still seemed strong. There was a little keyhole, and the chest was locked.

Sandy tried to pry it open, but the lock held firm.

Janet went out of the room and came back with one of her mother's hairpins.

She bent one end of the hairpin into a hook and pushed it into the keyhole. "Abracadabra," Janet said. "Open, Sesame!"

The lock clicked and sprang open. Janet lifted the lid of the little chest.

Inside were three buttons. One was black and shiny with a lot of little flat sides, like a diamond. The second was square. It glowed dark red and seemed to have a light far down inside it. The third was flat and round, bigger than the other two. It was milky in color and gleamed like a pearl.

"They're the Witch's prize buttons!" Sandy whispered.

16

"NO wonder Betsy liked to collect buttons," Janet said. "Aren't these beautiful?"

Sandy took the white button out of the chest and looked hard at it. She began to see things she hadn't noticed at first. As she looked they became more and more clear. "Janet," Sandy said, when she had been staring for some time at the button, "it's like a little flying saucer."

Now Janet took a good look. At first she too saw only a round flat pearly button. Then she saw port-holes, and a door.

Sandy held the button on her out-stretched palm. Before she knew what was happening it rose into the air and circled the room. It came to rest again on Sandy's hand.

"It *is* a flying saucer," Janet said.

Sandy laid the pearly button on the bed and picked up the square red button. She looked deep into it. The little light seemed to flicker. "This one sure is spooky," she said. "It must be magic too. I wonder what it's good for."

Janet was holding the black button. The shiny sides glittered and reflected colors from everything in the room. "It hardly seems to be black at all now," Janet said. "Maybe all this one does is change color. It's too bad the white button is only a toy. I wish we were the right size to fly in it."

Suddenly all the world seemed to turn pink. Sandy didn't know what was happening. Then she saw that she was sitting on top of a high cliff. "Get back, Janet!" Sandy scrambled away from the edge. The ground under her was soft and spongy.

"Yipe!" Janet looked down. She crawled over to Sandy.

The girls huddled together on the strange pink earth. They looked around. Sandy pointed. "There's the button space ship. Only now it's big enough for us to get into."

"You mean," Janet said, "now we're small enough. Don't you know we're still on my bed? Only now we're not much bigger than fleas."

It was true. The room seemed enormous. The brass chest looked as large as a house.

Sandy still had the square button in her hand. "This changed size too," she said, showing it to Janet.

Janet looked at the black button. "So did this one, maybe because we're holding them. Our clothes changed too."

"That's lucky," Sandy said. "I'm so small now I'd never be able to climb out of one of my shoes if it was its usual size."

Janet stood up. Her feet sank into the soft bedspread. It was difficult to walk but she made her way over to the button spaceship. "There ought to be some way to get in," she said. "I wish I knew what it was."

No sooner had Janet said this than she did know. She tapped three times on the side of the white button. A door opened in the space ship, and a ladder came down.

"Come on, Sandy." Janet started to climb the steps.

Sandy put the red button into the pocket of her jeans. She struggled to her feet and walked across the bedspread to the white button spaceship. Then she followed Janet up the ladder and into the flying saucer.

17

WHEN Sandy reached the top of the ladder she stepped into the spaceship. She turned around and lifted the ladder into the flying saucer. Each step folded as Sandy pulled it up. When she was done, the ladder was a neat stack just inside the door of the ship. Sandy closed the door.

Janet was looking out of a wide window. "This must be the windshield. There's a stick here that looks as if it's meant to steer the ship."

Two seats were placed side by side with the stick coming up from the floor between them. Janet and Sandy sat down. Janet took hold of the stick and pulled it up. The flying saucer rose into the air. When she pushed the stick forward the ship flew forward. And when she took her hand off the stick, the ship stood still. Janet practiced flying all around the room.

"My mother loves fresh air." Janet pointed to the window. It was open about two inches at the top. Janet steered the flying saucer through the window and out into the sunshine.

Sandy took a turn at the stick. It was easier to steer the spaceship than to ride a bicycle. At first the girls had a hard time telling what they were looking at. Everything was so big. Sandy tried flying very high. Then things began to look more like themselves.

"I'm beginning to know what the world is like to a mosquito," Sandy said.

She decided to fly home and see what was happening there. Her mother was just coming down the front steps with the baby carriage. An enormous Lisa was wearing her new snowsuit. When Mrs. James had walked to the end of the block and turned the corner, Sandy flew down toward the steps. She leveled off and steered the flying saucer through the mail slot in the front door and into the hall.

Sandy's father was sitting in the living room watching television. The New York Jets were playing the Green Bay Packers. Sandy knew that her father wouldn't see or hear anything else until halftime.

Zooming over her father's head, Sandy flew through the house to the kitchen. There was something on the kitchen table that looked like a note. The writing was so big that Sandy flew up to the ceiling and turned the flying saucer on edge so she and Janet could look through the windshield at the note.

Dear Sandy,
    I've taken Lisa to the park. Get yourself and Janet some lunch.
                Love,
                Mother

Sandy straightened the flying saucer and brought it down to land on the tabletop. She opened the door and pushed out the ladder. It unfolded. The girls walked down the steps.

"I smell cinnamon," Janet said.

Sandy saw a gigantic pan in the middle of the table. She ran over to it and looked up at the brown crust that hung over the edge of the pan far above her. "Apple pie," she said. "My mother must have found the Witch's apples."

"Yes," Janet said. She pointed to the

basket on the floor. "At least nobody seems to have eaten any yet."

"We'll have to do something," Sandy said. "But first let's have lunch. I can't think with an empty stomach."

They were much too small to open the refrigerator, but one of the kitchen cabinet doors was open a crack. They climbed back into the flying saucer and flew into the cabinet.

All the cereal and cracker boxes were closed tight, and the lid was on the jar of peanut butter.

"There are nuts in a bowl on the table," Sandy said.

Janet steered the flying saucer out of the cabinet and into the bowl. The girls again got out of the ship. They climbed across the nuts until they found an almond with a cracked shell. Sandy and Janet made their way through the crack.

It was like walking into a dark cave and nibbling on a rock.

"Now I know why mosquitoes eat people," Sandy said.

The girls picked their way out of the shell. Sandy looked across the wide table. On the other side of the pie she saw something yellow.

"Back into the spaceship, Janet," Sandy said. She started to sing, "You must never put bananas in the refrigerator."

18

EVEN tunneling through the skin of a banana was hard work for Janet and Sandy. They finally managed to tear a hole in one end. Now they could reach in and scoop out handfuls of the soft fruit. It was messy but they were hungry.

"I never ate so much banana in my life," said Janet after a while. "Now that I think of it, I never did like bananas very much."

"Don't complain, Janet." Sandy licked her fingers. "It's food. And anyway, you're my guest. You should be polite about what I serve you for lunch."

Janet wiped her hands on the smooth outside of the banana. "I've had enough," she said.

Just then the doorbell rang.

The Jets were trying for a touchdown. Mr. James never heard the doorbell.

The girls climbed back into the spaceship and flew to the front door. Sandy's father didn't look up. He was too busy watching the television.

Sandy was driving. She flew low and looked out of the mail slot. "I don't see anybody, Janet. They must have gone away." She steered the button spaceship through the slot and out into the open air.

They were flying over the front stoop when the flying saucer gave a jerk and stopped still. Sandy pushed the stick forward, but the spaceship stayed where it was. Suddenly it rose up higher. Again it stopped.

"Something's wrong, Janet," Sandy said. "I can't control it."

"Here. Let me take over." Janet grabbed the stick and shifted the flying saucer into reverse. It jiggled. Janet moved the stick back and forth. "It's just stuck," she said. Then the spaceship tipped on its side.

Sandy had a sudden, awful thought. "It's as if an invisible giant was holding the white button," she said. "Oh, Janet, do you suppose Silas could have kept one of the Witch's apples and eaten it?"

Janet stopped trying to drive the flying saucer. "We know Silas wanted to get his hands on the buttons. Remember what a mess he made in the old house when he was looking for them. Now we really are in trouble." Janet took the black button out of her pocket and rubbed it nervously.

Sandy bared her teeth like a tiger. "I

feel more and more like a mosquito. If only I could see Silas I'd pick a tender spot and bite."

Janet turned the black button over and over in her hand. "I wish we could see what's holding us," she said.

As soon as she said this the side portholes of the flying saucer became dark. Something was covering them. Sandy ran to see what it was.

"Fingers," she said. "I can see lines like a huge fingerprint." Sandy came back to her seat beside Janet. She didn't talk about biting any more now that she'd seen the big fingers. She remembered what can happen to a mosquito.

Neither of the girls wanted to talk now.

All at once the flying saucer was lifted even higher. Sandy and Janet looked through the windshield at an enormous greeny-blue eye.

"Witch Betsy!" Sandy gasped.

"She's alive," Janet said. "And she wants her buttons back."

Sandy pulled the square red button out of the pocket of her jeans. She looked at it. Deep inside the button the little light flickered. "This button is so small now that I don't think Betsy could even see it," Sandy said. "And she couldn't hear our voices no matter how loud we screamed. Anyway she has the door of the space ship jammed shut with her finger. What shall we do?"

Sandy heard a strange hollow voice. It seemed to come from far far down in the red button. "Use the Wishing Button, stupid," the voice said.

Sandy grabbed Janet's arm. "Did you hear that, Janet?" Sandy could hardly raise her voice to a whisper. "The red button talks!" she said. "It can answer questions."

Janet nodded. "Sandy," she said, "the red button is right. We are stupid." She held up the black button. It glittered like a diamond, each side flashing a different color. "We should have known. This is the Wishing Button. Every time I wished for something it came true." Janet closed her hand over the button. "Funny," she said, "now that I know it's a Wishing Button, I'm scared."

"Don't be scared, Janet," Sandy said. "Just think hard and make a good wish."

Janet closed her eyes and leaned her forehead against her fist. Then she took a deep breath, opened her eyes, and rubbed the black button. "I wish we were our right size and standing beside Witch Betsy on the doorstep."

19

THE Witch looked at Sandy and Janet. "I'm glad it was you who found the magic buttons," she said. "I hope you didn't get into trouble with them." She put the flying saucer button into a little black handbag. "Please, could I have the other two. They're not safe to play with."

Sandy looked at the red button. She had only just found out how to use it.

"If this one answers questions," she said, "it would be handy to have in school."

"A very good reason why you should give it back to me," the Witch said. She held out her hand. Sandy gave her the button. Betsy dropped it into her handbag.

"Please," Sandy begged, "could we use the Wishing Button before we give it back?"

Betsy looked shocked. "That's the most dangerous button of all! I have *never* used it."

"Then why do you keep it?" Janet asked.

"It's better for me to have it than somebody like Silas," Betsy said. "What do you want it for?"

"We have to do something about the apples Silas gave my mother," Sandy said. "My father always gets hungry at halftime when he's watching a football game. He's sure to take a piece of the apple pie mother made."

"What's wrong with that?" the Witch wanted to know. "Surely your father has a right to eat pie if he wants to. By the way, how did the cookies turn out?"

"Mother sewed the cooky you made to Lisa's snowsuit," Sandy said.

Betsy nodded. "I thought she would."

Sandy lost her temper. "Betsy!" she screamed. "It would be dangerous for my father to be invisible."

The Witch stared at her. "What in the world are you talking about?"

"The apples," Janet explained.

Betsy took a long look at Sandy. "Unless you steal them," she said, "there is nothing wrong with those apples."

Sandy felt guilty. She didn't know what to say.

Janet felt she had to say something to change the subject. "Betsy, why don't you rebuild your house with the Wishing Button?"

"Too easy," the Witch said. "There's no fun in that. Anyway I was getting tired of the place."

Sandy was still worried about the apples. "Why were *you* invisible?" she asked the Witch.

"A trick of the trade." Betsy vanished right before their eyes. Then slowly she came back into view. "Now, if you'll let me have that button you're holding, Janet, I'll be on my way."

Janet gave Betsy the glittering black Wishing Button. "I still have your brass chest," she said.

The Witch opened her bag and dropped the Wishing Button into it. "I don't need the chest anymore. I'm planning to take a trip. The chest would be just one more thing to take along. You and Sandy can keep it. Oh, and don't worry about Silas. He's taken a job in the trimming store. He'd been among buttons so long, he found he wasn't happy away from them."

Betsy started to walk down the steps. Then she turned and came back. She opened her handbag and took out a glass button. "Here's something to keep in the chest," she said. "I found it this morning in an antique store on Coney Island Avenue." Betsy handed the button to Sandy.

The two girls looked at the glass button. It was soft gray in color and shaped like a round ball. And it seemed to be filled with smoke.

"What's it good for?" Sandy asked.

Witch Betsy smiled. "I don't know," she said. "But I'm sure you and Janet will find a use for it."